ROALD DAHL'S REVOLTING RHYMES

with illustrations by
QUENTIN BLAKE

JONATHAN CAPE
LONDON

Other books for children
by the same author

CHARLIE AND THE CHOCOLATE FACTORY
JAMES AND THE GIANT PEACH
FANTASTIC MR FOX
THE MAGIC FINGER
CHARLIE AND THE GREAT GLASS ELEVATOR
THE WONDERFUL STORY OF HENRY SUGAR
BOY
GOING SOLO
MY YEAR

by the same author with illustrations by
Quentin Blake

DANNY, CHAMPION OF THE WORLD
THE ENORMOUS CROCODILE
THE TWITS
GEORGE'S MARVELLOUS MEDICINE
THE BFG
DIRTY BEASTS
THE WITCHES
THE GIRAFFE AND THE PELLY AND ME
MATILDA
ESIO TROT
THE MINPINS
REVOLTING RECIPES

Conditions of Sale
This book is sold subject to the condition that the Plates
therein, or any part of them, shall not, by way of trade or
otherwise, be made up for sale, or resold in any form
other than the form in which they are published.

First published in 1982
Reprinted 1982, 1983 (three times), 1984, 1985, 1987, 1996, 1998, 1999, 2001, 2002, 2004
Text copyright © Felicity Dahl and the other Executors
of the Estate of Roald Dahl 1988
Ilustrations © 1982 by Quentin Blake
Jonathan Cape Ltd
An imprint of Random House Children's Books
61-63 Uxbridge Road, London W5 5SA

British Library Cataloguing in Publication Data

Dahl, Roald
Roald Dahl's revolting rhymes.
I. Title II. Blake, Quentin
821'.914 PR6054. A35
ISBN 978 0 224 02932 2 (from January 2007)
0 224 02932 0

Printed in China

www.**kidsatrandomhouse**.co.uk/roalddahl
www.roalddahl.com

CINDERELLA

I GUESS you think you know this story.
You don't. The real one's much more gory.
The phoney one, the one you know,
Was cooked up years and years ago,
And made to sound all soft and sappy
Just to keep the children happy.
Mind you, they got the first bit right,
The bit where, in the dead of night,
The Ugly Sisters, jewels and all,
Departed for the Palace Ball,
While darling little Cinderella
Was locked up in the slimy cellar,
Where rats who wanted things to eat,
Began to nibble at her feet.
She bellowed, "Help!" and "Let me out!"
The Magic Fairy heard her shout.
Appearing in a blaze of light,
She said, "My dear, are you all right?"
"*All right?*" cried Cindy. "Can't you see
"I feel as rotten as can be!"
She beat her fist against the wall,
And shouted, "Get me to the Ball!
"There is a Disco at the Palace!
"The rest have gone and I am jalous!
"I want a dress! I want a coach!
"And earrings and a diamond brooch!
"And silver slippers, two of those!
"And lovely nylon panty-hose!
"Done up like that I'll guarantee
"The handsome Prince will fall for me!"
The Fairy said, "Hang on a tick."
She gave her wand a mighty flick
And quickly, in no time at all,
Cindy was at the Palace Ball!
It made the Ugly Sisters wince
To see her dancing with the Prince.
She held him very tight and pressed
Herself against his manly chest.
The Prince himself was turned to pulp,
All *he* could do was gasp and gulp.

Then midnight struck. She shouted, "Heck!
"I've got to run to save my neck!"
The Prince cried, "No! Alas! Alack!"
He grabbed her dress to hold her back.
As Cindy shouted, "Let me go!"
The dress was ripped from head to toe.
She ran out in her underwear,
And lost one slipper on the stair.
The Prince was on it like a dart,
He pressed it to his pounding heart,
"The girl this slipper fits", he cried,
"Tomorrow morn shall be my bride!
"I'll visit every house in town
"Until I've tracked the maiden down!"
Then rather carelessly, I fear,
He placed it on a crate of beer.
At once, one of the Ugly Sisters,
(The one whose face was blotched with blisters)

Sneaked up and grabbed the dainty shoe,
And quickly flushed it down the loo.
Then in its place she calmly put
The slipper from her own left foot.
Ah-ha, you see, the plot grows thicker,
And Cindy's luck starts looking sicker.
Next day, the Prince went charging down
To knock on all the doors in town.
In every house, the tension grew.
Who was the owner of the shoe?
The shoe was long and very wide.
(A normal foot got lost inside.)
Also it smelled a wee bit icky.
(The owner's feet were hot and sticky.)
Thousands of eager people came
To try it on, but all in vain.
Now came the Ugly Sisters' go.
One tried it on. The Prince screamed, "No!"
But she screamed, "Yes! It fits! Whoopee!
"So now you've got to marry me!"
The Prince went white from ear to ear.
He muttered, "Let's get out of here."
"Oh no you don't! You've made a vow!

"There's no way you can back out now!"
"Off with her head!" the Prince roared back.
They chopped it off with one big whack.
This pleased the Prince. He smiled and said,
"She's prettier without her head."
Then up came Sister Number Two,
Who yelled, "Now *I* will try the shoe!"
"Try this instead!" the Prince yelled back.
He swung his trusty sword and *smack* –
Her head went crashing to the ground.
It bounced a bit and rolled around.
In the kitchen, peeling spuds,
Cinderella heard the thuds
Of bouncing heads upon the floor,
And poked her own head round the door.
"What's all the racket?" Cindy cried.
"Mind your own bizz," the Prince replied.
Poor Cindy's heart was torn to shreds.
My Prince! she thought. He chops off *heads*!
How could I marry anyone
Who does that sort of thing for fun?
The Prince cried, "Who's this dirty slut?
"Off with her nut! Off with her nut!"
Just then, all in a blaze of light,
The Magic Fairy hove in sight,
Her Magic Wand went *swoosh* and *swish*!
"Cindy!" she cried, "come make a wish!
"Wish anything and have no doubt
"That I will make it come about!"
Cindy answered, "Oh kind Fairy,
"This time I shall be more wary.
"No more Princes, no more money.
"I have had my taste of honey.
"I'm wishing for a decent man.
"They're hard to find. D'you think you can?"
Within a minute, Cinderella
Was married to a lovely feller,
A simple jam-maker by trade,
Who sold good home-made marmalade.
Their house was filled with smiles and laughter
And they were happy ever after.

JACK AND THE BEANSTALK

JACK's mother said, "We're *stony broke*!
   "Go out and find some wealthy bloke
   "Who'll buy our cow. Just say she's sound
   "And worth at least a hundred pound.
"But don't you dare to let him know
"That she's as old as billy-o."
Jack led the old brown cow away,
And came back later in the day,
And said, "Oh mumsie dear, guess what
"Your clever little boy has got.
"I got, I really don't know how,
"A super trade-in for our cow."
The mother said, "You little creep,
"I'll bet you sold her much too cheap."
When Jack produced one lousy bean,
His startled mother, turning green,
Leaped high up in the air and cried,
"I'm *absolutely stupefied*!
"You crazy boy! D'you really mean
"You sold our Daisy for a bean?"
She snatched the bean. She yelled, "You chump!"
And flung it on the rubbish-dump.
Then summoning up all her power,
She beat the boy for half an hour,
Using (and nothing could be meaner)
The handle of a vacuum-cleaner.
At ten p.m. or thereabout,
The little bean began to sprout.
By morning it had grown so tall
You couldn't see the top at all.
Young Jack cried, "Mum, admit it now!
"It's better than a rotten cow!"
The mother said, "You lunatic!
"Where are the beans that I can pick?
"There's not *one bean*! It's bare as bare!"
"No no!" cried Jack. "You look up there!
"Look very high and you'll behold
"Each single leaf is solid gold!"
By gollikins, the boy was right!
Now, glistening in the morning light,

The dreaded words would come . . . And then . . .
From somewhere high above the ground
There came a frightful crunching sound.
He heard the giant mutter twice,
"By gosh, that tasted very nice.
"Although" (and this in grumpy tones)
"I wish there weren't so many bones."
"By Christopher!" Jack cried. "By gum!
"The Giant's eaten up my mum!
"He smelled her out! She's in his belly!
"I had a hunch that she was smelly."
Jack stood there gazing longingly
Upon the huge and golden tree.
He murmured softly, "Golly-gosh,
"I guess I'll *have* to take a wash
"If I am going to climb this tree
"Without the Giant smelling me.
"In fact, a bath's my only hope . . ."
He rushed indoors and grabbed the soap
He scrubbed his body everywhere.
He even washed and rinsed his hair.
He did his teeth, he blew his nose
And went out smelling like a rose.
Once more he climbed the mighty bean.
The Giant sat there, gross, obscene,
Muttering through his vicious teeth
(While Jack sat tensely just beneath)
Muttering loud, "FEE FI FO FUM,
"RIGHT NOW I CAN'T SMELL ANYONE."
Jack waited till the Giant slept,
Then out along the boughs he crept
And gathered so much gold, I swear
He was an instant millionaire.
"A bath", he said, "does seem to pay.
"I'm going to have one every day."

SNOW-WHITE AND THE SEVEN DWARFS

WHEN little Snow-White's mother died,
The king, her father, up and cried,
"Oh, what a nuisance! What a life!
"Now I must find another wife!"
(It's never easy for a king
To find himself that sort of thing.)
He wrote to every magazine
And said, "I'm looking for a Queen."
At least ten thousand girls replied
And begged to be the royal bride.
The king said with a shifty smile,
"I'd like to give each one a trial."
However, in the end he chose
A lady called Miss Maclahose,
Who brought along a curious toy
That seemed to give her endless joy –
This was a mirror framed in brass,
A MAGIC TALKING LOOKING-GLASS.
Ask it something day or night,
It always got the answer right.
For instance, if you were to say,
"Oh Mirror, what's for lunch today?"
The thing would answer in a trice,
"Today it's scrambled eggs and rice."
Now every day, week in week out,
The spoiled and stupid Queen would shout,
"Oh Mirror Mirror on the wall,
"Who is the fairest of them all?"

The Queen sat down and ate the heart!
(I only hope she cooked it well.
Boiled heart can be as tough as hell.)
While all of this was going on,
Oh where, oh where had Snow-White gone?
She'd found it easy, being pretty,
To hitch a ride in to the city,
And there she'd got a job, unpaid,
As general cook and parlour-maid
With seven funny little men,
Each one not more than three foot ten,
Ex horse-race jockeys, all of them.
These Seven Dwarfs, though awfully nice,
Were guilty of one shocking vice –
They squandered all of their resources
At the race-track backing horses.
(When they hadn't backed a winner,
None of them got any dinner.)
One evening, Snow-White said, "Look here,
"I think I've got a great idea.
"Just leave it all to me, okay?
"And no more gambling till I say."
That very night, at eventide,
Young Snow-White hitched another ride,
And then, when it was very late,
She slipped in through the Palace gate.
The King was in his counting house
Counting out his money,
The Queen was in the parlour
Eating bread and honey,
The footmen and the servants slept
So no one saw her as she crept
On tip-toe through the mighty hall
And grabbed THE MIRROR off the wall.
As soon as she had got it home,
She told the Senior Dwarf (or Gnome)
To ask it what he wished to know.
"Go on!" she shouted. "Have a go!"
He said, "Oh Mirror, please don't joke!
"Each one of us is stony broke!
"Which horse will win tomorrow's race,

And mud and mush and slush and slime.
Worse still, upon the heel of one
Was something that a dog had done.
I say once more, what *would* you think
If all this horrid dirt and stink
Was smeared upon your eiderdown
By this revolting little clown?
(The famous story has no clues
To show the girl removed her shoes.)
Oh, what a tale of crime on crime!
Let's check it for a second time.

Crime One, the prosecution's case:
She breaks and enters someone's place.

Crime Two, the prosecutor notes:
She steals a bowl of porridge oats.

Crime Three: She breaks a precious chair
Belonging to the Baby Bear.

Crime Four : She smears each spotless sheet
With filthy messes from her feet.

A judge would say without a blink,
"Ten years hard labour in the clink!"
But in the book, as you will see,
The little beast gets off scot-free,
While tiny children near and far
Shout, "Goody-good! Hooray! Hurrah!"
"Poor darling Goldilocks!" they say,
"Thank goodness that she got away!"
Myself, I think I'd rather send
Young Goldie to a sticky end.
"Oh daddy!" cried the Baby Bear,
"My porridge gone! It isn't fair!"
"Then go upstairs," the Big Bear said,
"Your porridge is upon the bed.
"But as it's inside mademoiselle,
"You'll have to eat *her* up as well."

LITTLE RED RIDING HOOD AND THE WOLF

As soon as Wolf began to feel
That he would like a decent meal,
He went and knocked on Grandma's door.
When Grandma opened it, she saw
The sharp white teeth, the horrid grin,
And Wolfie said, "May I come in?"
Poor Grandmamma was terrified,
"He's going to eat me up!" she cried.
And she was absolutely right.
He ate her up in one big bite.
But Grandmamma was small and tough,
And Wolfie wailed, "That's not enough!
"I haven't yet begun to feel
"That I have had a decent meal!"
He ran around the kitchen yelping,
"I've *got* to have a second helping!"
Then added with a frightful leer,
"I'm therefore going to wait right here
"Till Little Miss Red Riding Hood
"Comes home from walking in the wood."
He quickly put on Grandma's clothes,
(Of course he hadn't eaten those.)

Once more the maiden's eyelid flickers.
She draws the pistol from her knickers.
Once more, she hits the vital spot,
And kills him with a single shot.
Pig, peeping through the window, stood
And yelled, "Well done, Miss Riding Hood!"

Ah, Piglet, you must never trust
Young ladies from the upper crust.
For now, Miss Riding Hood, one notes,
Not only has *two* wolfskin coats,
But when she goes from place to place,
She has a PIGSKIN TRAVELLING CASE.